Books by Pat Rhoads Mauser

How I Found Myself at the Fair
A Bundle of Sticks
Rip-Off
Patti's Pet Gorilla

PATTI'S PET GORILLA

Patti's
Pet Gorilla

by Pat Rhoads Mauser

illustrated
by Diane Palmisciano

Atheneum   1987   New York

Atheneum
Macmillan Publishing Company
866 Third Avenue, New York, NY 10022

Type set by V & M Graphics, New York City
Printed and bound by Maple-Vale Manufacturing Group, Binghamton, N.Y.
Designed by Mary Ahern
First Edition

10   9   8   7   6   5   4   3   2   1

Library of Congress Cataloging-in-Publication Data

Mauser, Pat Rhoads. Patti's pet gorilla.

SUMMARY: Not having anything for "show-and-tell," Patti makes up
a pet gorilla and then is faced with the problem of showing it
to her friends.
[1. Imagination—Fiction.   2. Gorillas—Fiction.
3. Schools—Fiction]   I. Title
PZ7.M44583Pat   1987   [E]   86-20546
ISBN 0–689–31279-2

*To
the family on Sherman Street—Brenda,
Chuck, Mom, Dad,
and me*

P.M.

*To
R.J.F., with love*

D.P.

Contents

PATTI'S PET GORILLA

1.

Show-and-Tell

"HURRY UP, PATTI," Mom called. "You're going to be late for school."

Patti pulled the last of her toys out of her window seat and piled them in the middle of her room. "Just a minute," she said, "I have to find something for show-and-tell."

Her cat, Smokey, pawed at the arm of a little stuffed gorilla.

"Too bad I can't take you," Patti said to the cat. "You'd be better than that dumb magic trick David tried to do last week."

Mom poked her head into the room. "What a mess!" She picked up Patti's fuzzy bathrobe and hung it on the post of her canopy bed. "I wish you'd take better care of your clothes."

"I hate that thing Grandma made," Patti said. "Bathrobes are supposed to be pink or yellow, not brown."

Her mother frowned. "Grandma made it by hand—out of scraps. I'll bet this would make a wonderful show-and-tell."

"No," Patti said. "The boys would just laugh."

On her way to school Patti tried to find something, *anything*, for show-and-tell. She had already taken acorns

and yellow leaves. She had already taken smooth, gray rocks. Today she skipped through the park without picking up a thing. Nothing seemed just right.

Patti slid into her seat at school late. Show-and-tell had already started.

Hillary Walker was standing next to Mrs. Farley's desk. She held up a Barbie doll dressed in a ballet tutu.

"Dolls are stupid," Kevin Trent said, making an ugly face.

Hillary stuffed Barbie back into a paper sack and hurried to her seat.

Patti glared at Kevin. "I have a doll just like that," she said, "and I think she's pretty. You boys only like gross things, like dead bugs or snakes."

"Snakes are cool," Kevin said.

Mrs. Farley called on Tom Newberg next. He pulled up his pant leg to show a row of five black stitches.

Kevin clapped. No one laughed.

Tom sat down and Mrs. Farley looked around the room.

I hope she doesn't call on me, Patti thought. She crossed her fingers in her lap.

"What did you bring, Patti?" the teacher asked.

Patti swallowed. "I couldn't find anything," she said.

Mrs. Farley smiled. "Can you think of something to tell us, then?" She folded her hands on top of her desk and waited.

Patti's heart thumped in her chest. She hated having to think of things when everyone was watching. What could she tell them? Something terrific. Something even the boys would like.

Patti walked slowly to the front of

the classroom. She looked down at all the faces. Suddenly her mind went blank.

"Have you been on a trip lately?" Mrs. Farley asked, "Or do you have a special pet?"

"Well . . ."

Kevin laughed. He probably expected something ordinary, like a dog or cat.

"Well . . ." Patti's brain felt like mush. "Yes, I have a special pet." I do? she thought.

Everyone waited.

"What is it?" Mrs. Farley urged.

I don't know, Patti thought. What is it? She remembered the pile of toys in the middle of her bedroom.

"I have a pet . . . *gorilla*," she said.

2.

Patti's Pet Gorilla

KEVIN AND DAVID sat up straight.

"A gorilla?" Kevin said.

The boys liked it. "Sure. I've had him for years and years." In her mind Patti saw a black, fuzzy face with rubbery nostrils.

Mrs. Farley raised one eyebrow.

The faces in the classroom all looked toward Patti. A gorilla was something really good.

"What does he eat?" Kristin asked.

What in the world do gorillas eat? Patti wondered. "Well . . . lots of stuff."

"Bananas, I'll bet," David said.

"Yeah, bananas." Patti looked at Mrs. Farley, who sat with her arms folded across her chest. "We buy loads of them. Sometimes we get the ones with spots. They're cheaper."

"What's his name?" Hillary wanted to know.

Patti's face grew hot. They believed her story.

Maybe she could tell the class it was April Fool. In October? No, that wouldn't work. She had never known a gorilla. What kinds of names did they have?

The class was silent.

Patti pictured him with all her might. Her gorilla was six or seven feet tall with bushy, black fur. His eyes were round and shiny. His arms hung down to his knees. But he was a nice gorilla, big and shy like her uncle Bob.

"We call him Bob," Patti said.

Kevin's hand went to his forehead. "*Bob?*"

Mrs. Farley covered her mouth as if she were trying not to laugh. "That's a very strange name for a gorilla," she said.

Patti felt insulted. "No, it's not!" In her mind she saw Bob swinging from the top of her canopy bed. Although he really didn't exist, she was beginning to like Bob.

"Why don't you bring him to school?" David suggested.

"Yeah," Kevin agreed. "That's a great idea."

At this Mrs. Farley stood up. "I

think we've heard enough about Bob the gorilla," she said. "Will everyone please line up at the door? I think this is a good time for our nature walk."

Patti had heard enough about Bob, too. And she loved the weekly walks in the fresh air.

Mrs. Farley led the class through a quiet hall and outside into the autumn morning. The air felt crisp and cold, but the sun warmed Patti's back.

The class moved in twos down a sidewalk lined with maple trees. Everyone stopped to pick up the large yellow leaves that covered the walk.

Kevin climbed up a rough tree trunk. He sat on a branch and smiled down on the class.

"Okay, Kevin. Out of the tree," Mrs. Farley ordered.

Kevin grabbed the branch and swung down.

"Do you let Bob out to swing in the trees?" Hillary asked.

"Um . . . yes," she said, "but only when he's on the leash."

Oops! Bob couldn't swing in trees while he was on a leash. "You see, it's a *real long* leash," she explained.

Patti looked down the street. She could see the white fence in front of her own house just two blocks away. I sure hope we don't go down Sherman Street, she thought.

3.

Where's Bob?

AT THE CORNER was a little park with a dry wading pool. The pool was full of golden leaves and spiny chestnuts.

"Does Bob eat these?" Tom asked. He tossed a chestnut into the air and caught it.

How should I know? Patti thought. If a gorilla could peel a banana, he could probably open a chestnut, too.

Another story. Why couldn't they just forget about Bob?

But she thought about his trying to eat a chestnut, working the shell off with his hands and pricking himself. Poor Bob. What if he swallowed one, shell and all?

"We don't allow Bob to have chestnuts," Patti said.

The class continued through the park and down the sidewalk. Mrs. Farley pointed out an orange butterfly and an arrow of geese flying by overhead.

Patti looked again at her white fence. They were heading straight down Sherman Street, where she lived.

"Not this way," Patti said. But Mrs. Farley did not hear her.

What was she going to do? They were getting awfully close to her pet gorilla.

Mr. Gilmore looked up when the class walked past his fence. "Well, Patti," he said to his neighbor, "out on a field trip?"

"Sort of," Patti said. "Do you have anything in your yard for us to look at?" Anything to keep them away from her house.

Mr. Gilmore's mustache twitched. "How about a wasp's nest?"

Patti smiled.

Mrs. Farley nodded and unlatched the gate. "Class, I want to see hands in pockets."

"I don't have any pockets," Kristin said.

"Then pretend," the teacher answered.

Kristin placed her hands flat against the sides of her dress. She looked kind of funny, but there was

nothing wrong with pretending.

The class filed into Mr. Gilmore's backyard. They stood by the side of his house.

Stuck along the pointed part of the eaves was a round, gray nest with a little hole in the bottom. Everyone stood quietly, looking up.

"I don't see any wasps," David said.

"Maybe they flew south with the geese," Hillary said.

Patti kept her hands in her pockets, even though the wasp's nest was too high to reach. At seven feet tall, Bob could knock it off with one swipe, she thought proudly. In her imagination, Bob could do anything.

The class thanked Mr. Gilmore. Then they continued down the sidewalk on Sherman Street.

Patti's stomach turned upside down. She did not want to go any further. What would happen if the class found out there was no Bob?

Mrs. Farley stopped in front of a yellow house with white shutters. She reached over the fence to pull a cluster of orange berries off a tree. "This is called a mountain ash tree," she told the class.

Patti held her breath. She prayed no one would remember she lived here.

"Hey, Patti," David hollered. "Isn't this your house?"

"Um . . . yeah." Patti's hand went to her stomach. She knew what was coming next.

"Where's Bob?" several voices chimed.

Patti's face burned. Where *was* Bob?

She thought until her forehead hurt. The class would never believe he wasn't home right now, or that he was at the vet's. Where did gorillas go anyway?

4.

A Gorilla in the Bedroom

"HE'S IN MY BEDROOM," Patti said. She hoped this was the last story she would have to tell. "He's probably napping."

Hillary stood back. She craned her neck toward the upstairs bedroom. Everyone in the class squinted up at the window. Even Mrs. Farley shaded her eyes and looked.

Patti squirmed. There was no gorilla. The class would hate her when they found out. Bob was the best show-and-tell she'd ever had, but he wasn't even real.

"I see him!" Kevin shouted. He pointed toward the very center of Patti's bedroom window.

"No," Patti said. "I'm sure he's napping."

"I see him, too!" Hillary said. "I can see his arm and one eye."

Patti strained and tilted her head. There *was* a shadow in her bedroom. And a shiny eye that seemed to be looking right at her.

"But Bob naps all day long," Patti told the class.

"Why don't you put him on his leash and bring him outside?" said David.

Mrs. Farley looked down at Patti. "I think Bob would get scared if he saw so many children all at once."

"Yes . . . yes, he would." Patti let out her breath.

The class walked a few steps toward Mrs. Harkens' house.

Suddenly Kristin stopped short. "He moved! Bob's awake!" she squealed.

Kevin pointed.

Hillary jumped up and down. "Bob! Bob!" she called, and waved her arms.

Patti stared as the shadow moved. If that dark spot wasn't a real gorilla, then what could it be?

Mrs. Farley's eyes opened wide, but she didn't say anything.

Something big and dark and hairy was in Patti's room!

"But it's *not* my gorilla," Patti insisted. "It can't be. . . ." She strained her eyes once again. Now she could make out two big arms.

The spot seemed to move slowly past the window, ruffling Patti's pink curtains. Then it settled back near her bed.

Her heart pounded while the class stared at the dark shape. Patti stood still and blinked. It did not move again.

As the class walked back to school, Patti said softly to herself, "It wasn't a gorilla." And she tried to sound very sure. After all, you couldn't make something real simply by imagining it.

Could you?

5.

One Dark Eye

THE BELL RANG at three o'clock. The class lined up at the door.

"Can I come home with you?" Kevin wanted to know. "Maybe I could play with Bob."

"Um . . . no . . . I have a piano lesson," Patti said. Thank goodness she really did have a piano lesson. There was something in her room and she didn't know what it was.

Her mother picked her up outside the school.

"Did you go into my bedroom today?" Patti asked her.

"Your room is so messy, I don't think I could even get inside the door," her mother teased.

"Maybe I could sleep on the sofa tonight?"

Patti's mother laughed. "Or you could clean your room."

She hated playing the piano, but today Patti let her fingers move up and down the keys. She played "Crunchy Flakes" and "The Steamboat" over and over.

"How nice." Mrs. Simpson said, sounding pleased. "But time is up."

"Can't I play it one more time?" Patti begged.

Just then an older boy showed up

for his lesson. Finally, she was going to have to go home.

As her mother pulled the car into the driveway, Patti looked, but she couldn't see her window behind the mountain ash tree.

She went into the house and stood at the bottom of the stairs in the hallway. She listened for sounds coming from her room. If there was a gorilla . . . or something up there . . . he was being very quiet.

Patti placed one foot on the bottom stair. He could be waiting to surprise her.

"Go ahead," Mom said. "I want that mess cleaned up before dinner."

Should I tell Mom about Bob? Patti wondered. No, I'd get into trouble. She pulled her other foot up to the second stair.

Something rustled inside her room. Patti stood frozen. Was it going to jump out at her?

"Meow!" Smokey padded down the stairs.

Patti picked him up and hugged him to her chest.

"We're not scared, are we?" she said, and hurried up the rest of the stairs. But she stopped before peeking through the open door. There was no telling what a gorilla would do.

Smokey squirmed in Patti's arms. A dark shadow wiggled across the floor in front of her.

She held her breath and peered into her room.

"Oh, it's a shadow from the ash tree," she whispered to the cat.

The mound of toys still lay in the middle of her carpet. Her bathrobe

still hung on the bedpost. No gorilla seemed to be in the room.

She opened her closet door. No one was there, either.

Patti stood still and looked around. The only other hiding place was under her bed.

She held Smokey tightly and lifted her bedspread. There were socks and toys and books under the bed. But no gorilla.

She went to her window seat and turned around. What had the class seen from down below? Patti noticed the robe on the post of her canopy bed. The sleeves hung long and furry. One button shone near the collar.

As she looked, a breeze blew through the window. It ruffled the curtains and moved the sleeve of her brown bathrobe.

Patti stared at it, thinking, *Gorilla. My robe is the gorilla.* Moving in the breeze, the robe seemed to walk, and its button eyes sparkled. She laughed and looked into the eyes that stared back at her.

"Oh, it was only my bathrobe," Patti said, and she set Smokey down.

Then she pulled the robe off her bedpost and hugged it. "You aren't scary at all," she said.

And for a minute, Patti felt good. She could sleep in her own bed tonight. There was nothing hiding in her room after all.

But slowly a worry began to grow again. It grew until it filled her head.

Patti pinched her eyes shut.

What was she going to tell the class? They believed they saw a real gorilla. And there wasn't one. Patti sank down onto her bed. What was she going to do?

Her head began to ache and her stomach squeezed together. She should have taken acorns for show-and-tell. Acorns had never gotten her into trouble.

If only Bob could come to life— just for tomorrow. After all, he had been fun to think about. If he were just real for a day, he could go to school and meet her friends.

But Bob wasn't real. And Patti needed a good way to tell the truth.

She lay on her bed for a long time. Then suddenly Patti sat up straight. That's it, she thought! Bob *can* meet my friends!

6.

Bob Goes to School

THE NEXT MORNING Patti walked to school with her robe in a brown paper bag.

David rushed up to her. "Here," he said. "I have some bananas for Bob." They were bright yellow with no spots.

"Oh . . . thanks," Patti said. Her face burned as she hung them on the hook with her coat.

And Hillary showed up with a

knitted cap. "Bob might get cold now that he isn't living in the jungle anymore."

Tom brought a bright, new leash.

"Gee," Patti said, "I hope you didn't spend your allowance?"

Tom just smiled.

Then Mrs. Farley divided the class into groups. "Since everyone is so interested in gorillas," she said, "we're going to do a gorilla project."

"Wait a minute!" Patti said. Her heart flopped in her chest. Somehow this had to stop.

Patti walked to the front of the class with her paper bag. "Mrs. Farley, I have something for show-and-tell."

"That's nice," Mrs. Farley said, "but why don't you wait until Friday."

"I can't," Patti said. "This is important."

By now everyone was staring at Patti.

"Well . . . go ahead, then," Mrs. Farley said.

Patti swallowed and reached into her paper bag. She pulled out her brown, fuzzy robe and hung it on Mrs. Farley's yardstick. She hoped it looked just like it had on the post of her bed.

Tom laughed. "A bathrobe?"

"This is my . . . my grandmother made this. . . ." Patti tried to find the right words. "This is Bob, my pet gorilla," she said. Patti held her breath.

Mrs. Farley leaned forward at her desk. The kids in the class all looked at each other.

Patti fixed her robe just right with an arm sticking out and one button near the top. "See, it looks just like a gorilla."

Kevin turned his head first one way and then the other. He frowned.

"Hm," David said. "It does look like an animal, sort of."

Kristin's eyes widened. "I see it now. The top button is one of his eyes."

Suddenly everyone in the class could see Bob. And then they were all glaring at Patti.

"Shoot," Kevin said, "I thought you had a real gorilla."

"You said Bob ate bananas and walked around on a leash," David said, sounding cheated.

"Yeah," Hillary complained, "and what about swinging in trees? A bathrobe can't do that."

"I want my leash back," Tom said.

"I'm really sorry," Patti said to the class. She turned to Mrs. Farley. "It's just that I wanted something good for show-and-tell. And then everyone believed me."

"Stories have a way of getting bigger," Mrs. Farley told her.

Patti nodded. As big as a gorilla, she thought.

The teacher took another look at Bob. "I'll have to admit, with a little imagination, your robe does look like an animal."

Patti remembered being afraid to go into her room. She had almost believed her own tale.

"I even saw him move," Kristin said.

"That's stupid," Kevin said. But after a moment he started to laugh. "I guess I saw him, too," he confessed.

Then Tom laughed. Soon the whole class was looking at Patti's bathrobe and laughing. Even Mrs. Farley.

PATTI WENT HOME SMILING. "This was the best show-and-tell I've ever had," she said to herself.

And she was still smiling that night when she undressed and put on her furry, brown bathrobe.

Then she went down the hall . . . with Bob . . . to brush her teeth.